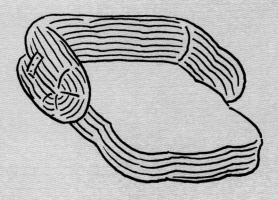

ALESSANDRO BECCHI
Italian
"Anfibio" sofa 1971

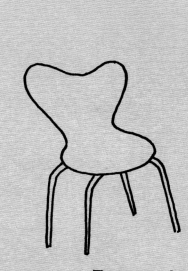

"Series 7" chair 1955

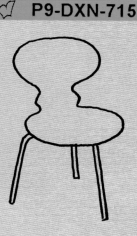

ARNE JACOBSEN
Danish
"Ant" sidechairs 1952-55

ISAMU NOGUCHI
American
Chess table 1947

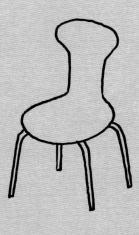

ALVAR AALTO
Finnish
"Savoy" vase 1936

TERENCE CONRAN
British
"Chequers" fabric 1951

ARNE JACOBSEN
Danish
"Egg" chair 1957

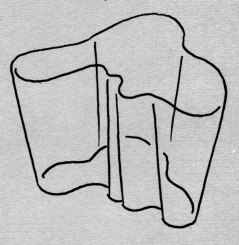

**STYLE OF
DE PAS, D'URBINO,
LOMAZZI**
Italian
"Blow" bed 1967

To Joseph Eichler and Milton Miller, two modernist uncles with great taste

Acknowledgments
I would like to thank Jacques Binsztok, Brigitte Morel, Howard Reeves, Feodor Rojankovsky, les Trois Ourses, Hugo Weinberg, Lia Ronnen, Florence Barrau, Chris Gash, and Tamara Petrosino.

Artist's Note
I use a brush and India ink to give the line a fat, luscious quality, and to allow me to vary the line from very thin to very thick. I also use India ink to create the black background. On the back, I draw with an opaque, pastel-colored pen. I fill in areas—first outlined in black—with Winsor & Newton watercolors, which I mix to achieve the palette I want.

Original hand-lettered font created by Steven Guarnaccia

The Library of Congress has cataloged the first U.S. edition of this book as follows:

Guarnaccia, Steven.
Goldilocks and the three bears / retold and illustrated by Steven Guarnaccia.
p. cm.
Summary: Illustrations featuring elements of the modernism movement in art provide a new look to this traditional tale of the uninvited visit of a young girl to the home of a family of bears. Includes a list of designers.
ISBN 0-8109-4139-2
[1. Bears Folklore. 2. Folklore.] I. Goldilocks and the three bears. English. II. Title.
PZ8.1.G933Go 2000
398.22dc21 99-35493

ISBN of this edition: 978-0-8109-8966-5

© Steven Guarnaccia
© Maurizio Corraini srl
All rights reserved to Maurizio Corraini srl Mantova
First Italian edition by Maurizio Corraini srl 1999
Original title: Riccioli d'oro e i tre orsi

Printed and bound in Italy
10 9 8 7 6 5 4 3 2 1

Abrams Books for Young Readers are available at special discounts when purchased in quantity for premiums and promotions as well as fundraising or educational use. Special editions can also be created to specification. For details, contact specialmarkets@abramsbooks.com or the address below.

THE ART OF BOOKS SINCE 1949
115 West 18th Street
New York, NY 10011
www.abramsbooks.com

GOLDILOCKS and the THREE BEARS

A Tale Moderne

Retold and illustrated by Steven Guarnaccia

Abrams Books for Young Readers, New York

Once upon a time,
a family of bears
lived in a split-level
house deep in the forest.
There was a big burly Papa Bear,
a medium-sized Mama Bear, and
their pint-sized Baby Bear.

And in their house was a chair for each of them: a big burly chair for Papa Bear, a medium-sized chair for Mama Bear, and a pint-sized chair for Baby Bear.

Upstairs they each had a bed. There was a big burly bed for Papa Bear, a medium-sized bed for Mama Bear, and a pint-sized bed for Baby Bear.

One day, Mama Bear
made chili for lunch.

There was a big burly bowl
for Papa Bear, a medium-sized bowl
for Mama Bear, and a pint-sized
bowl for Baby Bear.

The chili was piping hot, so the bears decided to go for a ramble in the woods while it cooled down.

Before long, a little girl named
Goldilocks came to the bears' house
and rapped on the front door.
There was no answer, but as she
was a curious young girl, she
let herself in to look around.

Goldilocks immediately spied the
three chairs. She climbed up
into the big burly chair,
but it was hard as a rock.

Next, she tried
to get comfortable
in the
medium-sized
chair, but it was
way too soft.

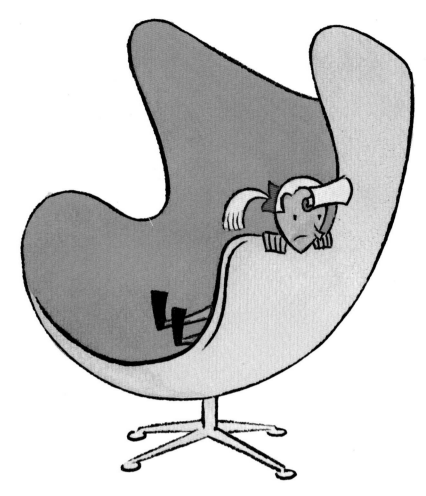

Finally, she
tried the
pint-sized chair,
and it fit her
perfectly.
But just as
she was getting
cozy, the chair
broke into pieces.

Before long, Goldilocks smelled the chili. She realized how hungry she was, so she tasted a spoonful from the big burly bowl. It was so hot she burned her tongue. Then she tried the chili in the medium-sized bowl. It was too chilly.

But when she tasted the chili in the pint-sized bowl, it was just the way she liked it, and she licked the bowl clean.

The warm food made Goldilocks
sleepy, so she went upstairs
to lie down.

First she tried the big burly bed, but it was too hard.

The medium-sized bed was too soft.

But when she lay down in the
pint-sized bed, it was just right,
and she fell asleep immediately.

Not long after, the bears,
done with their walk, made
their way home to eat lunch.

When Papa Bear entered the house,
he noticed something was wrong.
"Humph! Someone's been sitting in my
chair!" he said.

"Oh, fur and honey! Someone's been
sitting in my chair, too!" said Mama Bear.
"Oh, rats! Someone's been sitting in
my chair, and has smashed it to
smithereens!" said Baby Bear.

When Papa Bear sat down to eat,
he said with a gravelly growl, "Harumph!
Somebody's been eating my chili!"
Mama Bear looked at her bowl and the
spoon with chili on it.
"Someone's been eating my chili!" she said.
Baby Bear said, "It's so unfair! Someone's
been eating my chili, and has
eaten it all up."

Now the three bears grumbled,

clattered, and bopped up the stairs.

"Grr, someone's been sleeping in my bed!"
growled Papa Bear.
"Buzz fuzz! Someone's been sleeping in
my bed," said Mama Bear.

"Gee whillikers!" said Baby Bear.
"Someone's been sleeping in my bed,
and she's still there!"

Goldilocks woke with a start and saw
the three bears standing there, looking
down at her curiously.
"Yikes!" she said. Goldilocks bounced
out of Baby Bear's bed, down the stairs,
and out the door. She ran off toward
her home, and never set foot in that
part of the forest again.

POUL HENNINGSEN
Danish
"PH5" lamp 1958

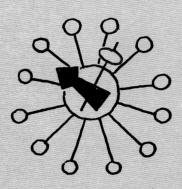

GEORGE NELSON
American
"Atom" clock 1949

GIO PONTI
Italian
spoon 1951

ALVIN LUSTIG
American
"Incantation" Fabric
1946-1947

GEORGE NELSON
American
"Asterisk" clock 1950

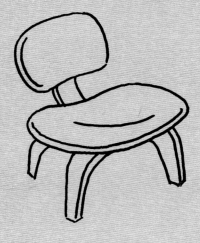

CHARLES RENNIE MACKINTOSH
Scottish
"Ladderback" chair 1902

CHARLES & RAY EAMES
American
"LCW" chair 1946

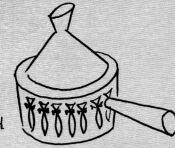

MARIANNE WESTMAN
Swedish
"Picknick" casserole 1956

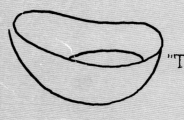

EVA ZEISEL
Hungarian
"Town & Country" pottery 1947

GEORGE NELSON
American
"Kite" clock 1953